Contents

Chapter One

Nancy lived a naughty life deep in the
forest in the land of Trittledore.

I AM READING

Sniffer and Naughty Nancy

ROGER ABBOTT

Illustrated by
COLIN WEST

KINGFISHER

KINGFISHER

This edition published by Kingfisher 2008
First published 2006 by Kingfisher
an imprint of Macmillan Children's Books
a division of Macmillan Publishers Limited
20 New Wharf Road, London N1 9RR
Basingstoke and Oxford
Associated companies throughout the world

www.panmacmillan.com

ISBN 978 0 7534 1691 4

Text copyright © Roger Abbott and Colin West 2006
Illustrations copyright © Colin West 2006

The right of Roger Abbott and Colin West to be identified as the
authors of this work has been asserted by them in accordance
with the Copyright, Designs and Patents Act 1988.

1 3 5 7 9 8 6 4 2
1TR/0408/WKT/(CHR)/115MA/C

A CIP catalogue record for this book is available from the British Library.

Printed in China

Nancy shared her tumbledown cottage with her pet dog named Sniffer.

Sniffer was a special dog, a bloodhound, who had a nose like a ripe, golden tomato.

Naughty Nancy loved all things that glittered. She had trained Sniffer to sniff out anything made of gold.

Every night, Nancy and her bloodhound would sneak off in search of new golden objects.

Nancy would release Sniffer and he would follow the scent of gold.

Sniffer always returned with something shiny and valuable, which Nancy put in her sack.

Nancy would carry the new treasures
home to her cottage. Her cupboards
were crammed with golden goodies.

8

There were golden necklaces, golden candlesticks, golden goblets, golden plates, golden teapots, golden coins, golden rings, golden earrings, golden bracelets, golden brooches, golden trinkets, golden thimbles, and even a golden dog bowl!

Chapter Two

Now one day in the land of Trittledore, the old king died. His handsome son was declared the new king.

A new crown was made for the occasion. It was studded with the finest jewels and made with the shiniest gold.

There were celebrations throughout the land and everyone admired the new king's splendid treasure.

People could not stop talking about his beautiful new crown, so word spread throughout the land.

It was not long before Naughty Nancy also heard the news about the king's priceless crown. She became jealous. "I'm going to make that crown my own," she said.

Chapter Three

Naughty Nancy found an old map of the castle and placed it under Sniffer's nose to show him where they were going.

Sniffer gave it several deep sniffs then wagged his tail. Then they waited for night to come.

When the sky had turned black they crept to the edge of the woods where they could see the king's castle. Sniffer caught the scent of gold in his nostrils.

Sniffer crept up to the castle and dived into the moat.

He doggy-paddled carefully across the water.

Then he climbed up the bank on the other side.

He spied an open window and scrambled inside the castle.

Sniffer followed the scent of gold.

His muddy paws took him up a flight

of steps.

He went along
a corridor, past
the royal
bathroom and
into the king's
bedroom itself...

He carefully picked the crown up in
his mouth and crept out of the room.

Sniffer scampered past some sleeping guards then doggy-paddled back across the moat again.

Naughty Nancy was waiting for him at the edge of the forest. She clapped her hands in glee when she saw the golden crown in Sniffer's jaws.

She placed it firmly on her head and
jumped for joy.

The crown really was hers!

Her naughty plan had worked.

So Naughty Nancy danced all the
way home.

Chapter Four

The next morning, Naughty Nancy awoke with the crown still on her head. She admired herself in the mirror. "It's so beautiful!" she sighed.

"Now I just need to brush my hair to show off its beauty even more."

Nancy grasped the crown and tried to remove it, but she couldn't. It was stuck. She tugged and tugged, then tugged again even harder, but it just would not budge. "Fiddlesticks!" she said.

"I need your help, Sniffer," said Nancy.
Sniffer held the crown in his jaws and
pulled hard. But he could not get it off.

"Goosepimples," Nancy muttered.

"What can I try next?"

Nancy wedged the crown in the door
and pulled with all her strength.
She turned this way and that way but
still it would not come off.

Just then Sniffer started barking loudly.
"What's the matter?" Nancy asked.

Naughty Nancy peered through the window to see if anyone was outside. To her horror she saw the king's soldiers. They were heading towards the cottage.

Chapter Five

Nancy grabbed a towel and wrapped it around her head. She wanted to hide the stolen crown.

Suddenly there was a loud knock at the door.

Nancy nervously opened the door.

A big soldier stood before her.

"The king's crown has been stolen!"

he snapped.

Nancy's knees started knocking.

"We followed some muddy paw prints from the king's bedroom which led us to your house," he added. Nancy's knees knocked even more.

Then the soldier spotted all the golden objects in Nancy's cottage. "What a lot of gold you have," he observed.

Sniffer started to snivel.

Then the soldier spied Nancy's bloodhound. "And what a big nose for a dog!"

Sniffer snivelled even more.

The soldier looked suspicious.

"Do you happen to know where the crown is?" he demanded.

Naughty Nancy felt scared and wasn't sure how to reply.

She shook
her head
repeatedly...

...but as she did so...

...the towel
slipped from
her head.

"Aha!" cried the soldier as the crown was revealed. "There it is!"

And so he arrested Nancy and Sniffer on the spot. Nancy knew there was no escape.

Chapter Six

Naughty Nancy and Sniffer were
taken to the castle and were brought
before the king. Nancy hung her head
low in shame.

The handsome king arose from his throne and stepped towards Nancy.

"Ah, my most precious treasure!" the king sighed. "How lovely, how wonderful, how beautiful!"

But the king was not talking about his crown, he was talking about Nancy.

"I have found my lost treasure," he announced, "and she who wears it I desire even more. Please will you marry me?"

Nancy didn't need to be asked twice.
She nodded her head to accept his
proposal. She liked the idea of getting
married to someone so handsome and
regal.

So Naughty Nancy stopped being naughty. She realized what a bad person she had been. She was truly sorry and returned all her stolen things. But the magnificent crown was forever stuck on her head.

The king had a new crown made for himself that matched Naughty Nancy's. And they lived together happily ever after.

And as for Sniffer... well, he got a job guarding the crown jewels!